THIS WALKER BOOK BELONGS TO:

_____

_____

_____

To Alice

First published 1990 by Walker Books Ltd
87 Vauxhall Walk, London SE11 5HJ

This edition published 2006

2 4 6 8 10 9 7 5 3 1

© 1990 Martin Baynton

The right of Martin Baynton to be identified as author/illustrator of this work has
been asserted by him in accordance with the Copyright, Designs and Patents Act 1988

This book has been typeset in Optima

Printed in China

British Library Cataloguing in Publication Data:
a catalogue record for this book is available from the British Library

ISBN-13: 978-1-4063-0526-5,
ISBN-10: 1-4063-0526-X

www.walkerbooks.co.uk

the DRAGON'S PURPOSE

Martin Baynton

WALKER BOOKS
AND SUBSIDIARIES
LONDON · BOSTON · SYDNEY · AUCKLAND

The courtyard was a mess. There were just three days to go before the midsummer carnival, and everyone was busy with the preparations.

Everyone but Jane.

Jane put on her armour, saddled her pony, and rode out through the castle gates.

She had an appointment to keep. With a dragon.

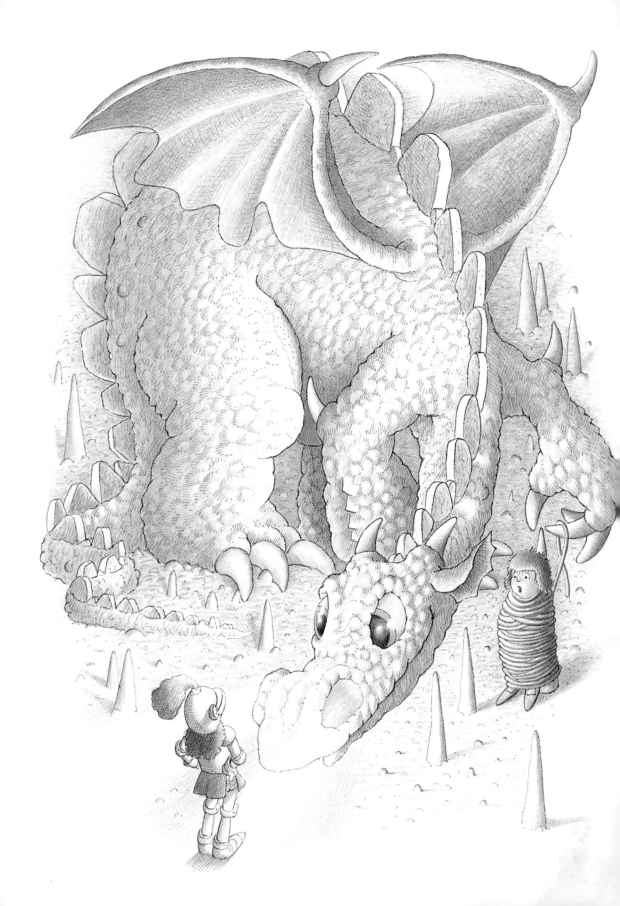

Jane was a knight. Not a pretend knight, but a fully qualified, highly trained Knight of the King's Guard.

The King himself had appointed her, when Jane had saved his son from a giant green dragon.

Jane had not killed the dragon. She had made friends with him. Now she was on her way to see him again; for it was Saturday, and she always visited him on a Saturday.

The ride to the dragon's mountain was hot and dusty. There had been no rain for many weeks and all the rivers were dry. Yet when she came to the dragon's cave, Jane found a new stream flowing beside it. She was very surprised, but too thirsty to wonder where it came from. She dismounted and took a drink. PAAAAAHH! The water was salty; like seawater, or tears. Oh dear, thought Jane, and she followed the stream to its giant green source.

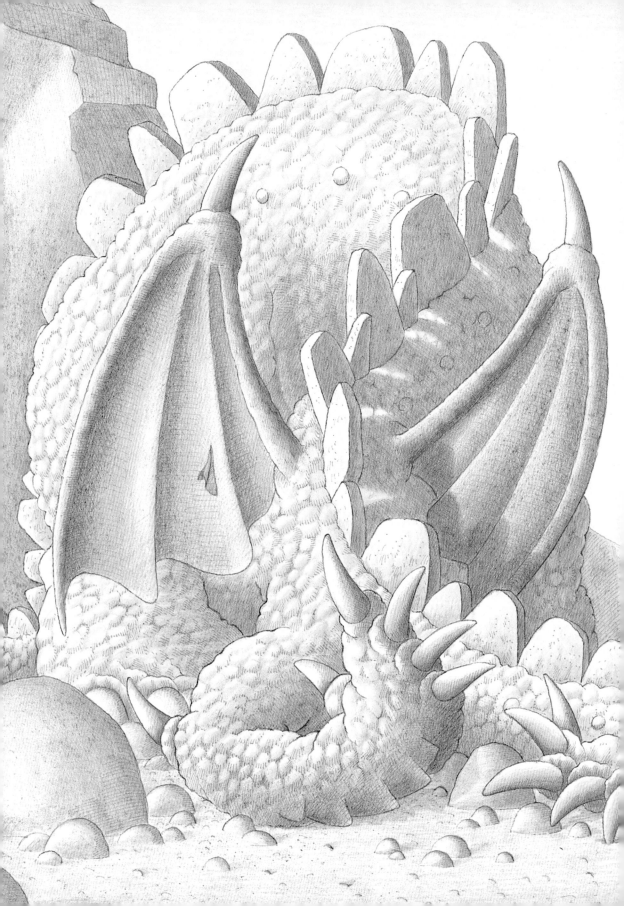

"Aren't you happy to see me?" asked Jane.

The dragon smiled and wiped his eyes. "I'm always happy to see you. I love Saturdays. But the rest of the week is so empty."

"Why?" said Jane.

"Because I'm a giant green dragon. I was born to scare people. All that changed when I met you. Now I don't know what to do with my life."

"I shall think of something," said Jane. "Now let's enjoy the day before I start crying too."

The dragon brightened up at once. He spread his spiky brown wings and let Jane climb onto his back. "Hold tight," he roared, and they rose up into the clear morning sky.

Everyone was still hard at work when Jane arrived back at the castle.

They asked Jane to help, but she wanted to be on her own. She was worried about the dragon and needed time to think.

Jane wandered through to the palace gardens. The court magician was there, standing among the dry and thirsty flowers.

He was trying out a new rain-making spell. It was not working.

Jane told him all about the dragon's empty life.

"He needs a new job, does he?" sighed the magician. "Well, so will I if I don't make a good spell of rain soon. Now stand back, this could be a big one."

Lightning crackled from the magician's hands and a tiny cloud drifted up from his hat, but no rain fell.

So Jane went to see her best
friend, the court jester. She told
him all about the unhappy dragon.
The jester listened carefully, and
shook his head.

"Your dragon was born to scare
people. That's what he was good at.
Then he met you. Though you didn't
mean to, you took something
important from him."

"What?" asked Jane sadly.

"You took away his purpose;
his special place in the world.
He needs a new purpose now.
Something only he can do.
And you must help him find it."

Jane felt miserable. She went to her quarters and sat down on the floor.

She could think of so many jobs the dragon might do. Yet none of them seemed quite right, none of them suited the nature of a giant green dragon.

The other knights were building their float for the carnival parade.

"Don't sit there moping," said the captain, "we need your help. The theme for the parade is 'Hallowe'en', but we can't think of anything scary enough for our float."

Jane leapt to her feet and danced a little dance.

"That's it," she cried, "that is IT!"

"What is what?" asked the captain.

"That is the answer to my problem, and yours," said Jane. "I think we'll have the scariest float in the world."

The day of the carnival arrived, and crowds lined the road to watch the main event: the Hallowe'en parade.

There were dozens of scary floats, each one more frightening than the last.

Right at the very end came Jane , the jester, and the knights.

Their float was an enormous nest, and in the nest sat a giant blue egg.

The judges laughed when they saw the egg.

"What's so scary about that?" they asked.

Jane smiled a secret smile and whispered into the nest.

With a magnificent roar, the giant green dragon burst from his hiding place and snorted a jet of hot flames over the heads of the judges.

The judges were terrified. One dived under the table. One fell backwards off his chair. A third just sat there sucking his thumb like a small child.

Jane clambered up beside the dragon.

"How do you feel now?" she asked.

"Better," laughed the dragon, "much, much better."

The dragon won first prize. And when the crowd saw how gentle he really was, they came to pat him and asked to ride on his back.

The dragon agreed, though his heart wasn't in it.

"I'm not a little kitten," he said to Jane. "I'm a giant green dragon born to scare people."

"And you did scare them," said Jane.

"Only for a moment," sighed the dragon, "and it was a sham; a piece of theatre. Thank you for trying to help, but this was never my purpose. I'm not an entertainer."

And he flew away without saying goodbye.

The next few days dragged by. There was still no sign of rain and all the royal flowers were dying.

The King lost his temper; the magician lost his job; and the jester lost his sense of humour.

Jane carried on with her duties, but all she could think about was the unhappy dragon.

Each evening she walked the battlements and stared across to the dragon's mountain.

Then, late one evening, she looked up and felt rain on her face.

"I've done it," boomed a happy voice. "I've found my purpose." It was the dragon.

"Climb up, climb up," he laughed as he landed next to Jane, "I'll show you."

Jane and the dragon flew to a distant cloud. The dragon beat his wings and drove the cloud forward like a boat in the wind.

"Watch this," he roared as they passed back over the palace gardens. He took a mighty breath and blew flame into the heart of the cloud.

It burst in a shower of raindrops.

"See that!" bellowed the dragon. "I scared the rain right out of it! I'm a giant green dragon born to scare rainclouds."

Jane laughed and hugged his neck. She was very wet and very happy, and the rain on her face disguised her quiet tears.

About the author...

Martin Baynton wanted to reverse the traditional treatment of fairytale heroines with this story. He says, "Fairy tales are tough on girls. Within their cruel pages, girls scrub floors, eat poisoned apples, sleep for centuries and are only saved when a handsome prince arrives to sweep them off their blistered knees into a world of Happily Ever After. Not so Jane. Jane saves herself and she most definitely does not want to live happily ever after. She wants adventure, danger, challenge – and 'happy' just isn't enough."

Martin has been a writer and illustrator since 1980 and has an international reputation for his books for children. He has recently partnered with the Academy award-winning Weta Workshop (The Lord of the Rings trilogy) and the Canadian children's television producers, Nelvana, to create a stunning animated television series based on the books, using the latest digital effects technology.

As well as writing and illustrating picture books for children, Martin also writes for the stage, television, film and radio. He was born in the UK and now lives in New Zealand.